OWL
MOON

I was born and grew up in New York City. Before I met my husband David Stemple, I thought birds were either pigeons or they weren't. But he grew up in the West Virginia mountains and knew a thing or three about birding.

So when we met, married, and moved to Massachusetts to raise a family, he began my slow education in the fine art of identifying birds. Our children grew up within the bird-watching culture and they are much better birders than I will ever be. But I sure do know my owls.

David took all three of our children owling, but the one in *Owl Moon* is our daughter, Heidi, who went on her father's very last owling expedition. On Christmas bird count night in 2006, he led a team of birders to a new record of screech and great horned owls in our small Western Massachusetts town.

Before I wrote *Owl Moon*, owling was the sort of thing that birders knew about but other people didn't. But now every week I hear of fathers and mothers and teachers and other grown-ups going out owling with their children. And the children all know, because of the book, that when you go owling, you have to be quiet and make your own warmth. That you have to look and listen. And that sometimes—like in everything else in life— sometimes there's an owl, and sometimes there isn't. It's the journey that is important. That and your companions along the way.

Jane Yolen

—Phoenix Farm

I am often asked why I think *Owl Moon* seems to have become a classic.

I don't know why! At least, I can't think of a single reason for it—I can, however, think of a number of reasons. One reason might be that it's a real-life adventure, and one that can be experienced by a young child. I went on adventures like this with my children in our woods, and I learned that Jane Yolen's husband, David, went on these adventures with their children.

Second, *Owl Moon* is told in the voice of the child. That's a *child*, not a boy or girl. Bundled up for a night in the woods, who could tell gender? *Child* seems to include every young person reading the book, no matter what their gender might be.

Third, it's classical, containing elements of mystery and journey. A trip to an unknown world in search of a mysterious creature: a coming-of-age journey and quest in one.

Fourth: its popularity might be that there is a positive father who leads with authority but at a child's pace, and who lends a hand when necessary. Sharing knowledge and experience with children is the aim of parenting, isn't it? It's opening the world to them and what could be better? I've always felt that way.

The last picture has the couple—father and child—heading back to home and warmth. I remember often carrying my son or daughter home when they became tired. That's security and love in one. My children always claimed the lighted window was in their room.

There are some extras I put in the pictures: animals hidden in the woods. I thought I hid them well, but didn't realize that kids saw every one—and at once. I suppose it is still fun to find them.

Maybe it was just the love of children and nature and adventure that Jane expressed so poetically, and that I identified with instantly.

OWL
MOON

by Jane Yolen

illustrated by John Schoenherr

Philomel Books   New York

Text copyright © 1987 by Jane Yolen.
Illustrations copyright © by John Schoenherr.
All rights reserved. Published by Philomel Books,
a division of Penguin Young Readers Group,
345 Hudson Street, New York, NY 10014.
Published simultaneously in Canada.
Manufactured in China
by South China Printing Co. Ltd.
Book design by Nanette Stevenson.

Library of Congress Cataloging-in-Publication Data
Yolen, Jane,   Owl Moon.
Summary: On a winter's night under a full moon, father and
daughter trek into the woods to see the Great Horned Owl.
[1. Owls–Fiction.   2. Fathers and daughters–
Fiction]   I. Schoenherr, John, ill.   II. Title.
PZ7.Y780w   1987   [E]   87-2300
ISBN 978-0-399-24799-6

10 9 8 7 6 5 4 3 2 1

For my husband, David,
who took all of our children owling —J.Y.

To my granddaughter, Nyssa,
for when she is old enough to go owling. —J.S.

It was late one winter night,
long past my bedtime,
when Pa and I went owling.
There was no wind.
The trees stood still
as giant statues.
And the moon was so bright
the sky seemed to shine.
Somewhere behind us
a train whistle blew,
long and low,
like a sad, sad song.

I could hear it
through the woolen cap
Pa had pulled down
over my ears.
A farm dog answered the train,
and then a second dog
joined in.
They sang out,
trains and dogs,
for a real long time.
And when their voices
faded away
it was as quiet as a dream.
We walked on toward the woods,
Pa and I.

Our feet crunched
over the crisp snow
and little gray footprints
followed us.
Pa made a long shadow,
but mine was short and round.
I had to run after him
every now and then
to keep up,
and my short, round shadow
bumped after me.

But I never called out.
If you go owling
you have to be quiet,
that's what Pa always says.

I had been waiting
to go owling with Pa
for a long, long time.

We reached the line
of pine trees,
black and pointy
against the sky,
and Pa held up his hand.
I stopped right where I was
and waited.
He looked up,
as if searching the stars,
as if reading a map up there.
The moon made his face
into a silver mask.
Then he called:
"Whoo-whoo-who-who-who-whooooooo,"
the sound of a Great Horned Owl.
"Whoo-whoo-who-who-who-whooooooo."

Again he called out.
And then again.
After each call
he was silent
and for a moment we both listened.
But there was no answer.
Pa shrugged
and I shrugged.
I was not disappointed.
My brothers all said
sometimes there's an owl
and sometimes there isn't.

We walked on.
I could feel the cold,
as if someone's icy hand
was palm-down on my back.
And my nose
and the tops of my cheeks
felt cold and hot
at the same time.
But I never said a word.
If you go owling
you have to be quiet
and make your own heat.

We went into the woods.
The shadows
were the blackest things
I had ever seen.
They stained the white snow.
My mouth felt furry,
for the scarf over it
was wet and warm.
I didn't ask
what kinds of things
hide behind black trees
in the middle of the night.
When you go owling
you have to be brave.

Then we came to a clearing
in the dark woods.
The moon was high above us.
It seemed to fit
exactly
over the center of the clearing
and the snow below it
was whiter than the milk
in a cereal bowl.

I sighed
and Pa held up his hand
at the sound.
I put my mittens
over the scarf
over my mouth
and listened hard.
And then Pa called:
"Whoo-whoo-who-who-who-whooooooo.
Whoo-whoo-who-who-who-whooooooooo."
I listened
and looked so hard
my ears hurt
and my eyes got cloudy
with the cold.
Pa raised his face
to call out again,
but before he could
open his mouth
an echo
came threading its way
through the trees.
"Whoo-whoo-who-who-who-whooooooo."

Pa almost smiled.
Then he called back:
"*Whoo-whoo-who-who-who-whoooooooo,*"
just as if he
and the owl
were talking about supper
or about the woods
or the moon
or the cold.
I took my mitten
off the scarf
off my mouth,
and I almost smiled, too.

The owl's call came closer,
from high up in the trees
on the edge of the meadow.
Nothing in the meadow moved.
All of a sudden
an owl shadow,
part of the big tree shadow,
lifted off
and flew right over us.
We watched silently
with heat in our mouths,
the heat of all those words
we had not spoken.
The shadow hooted again.

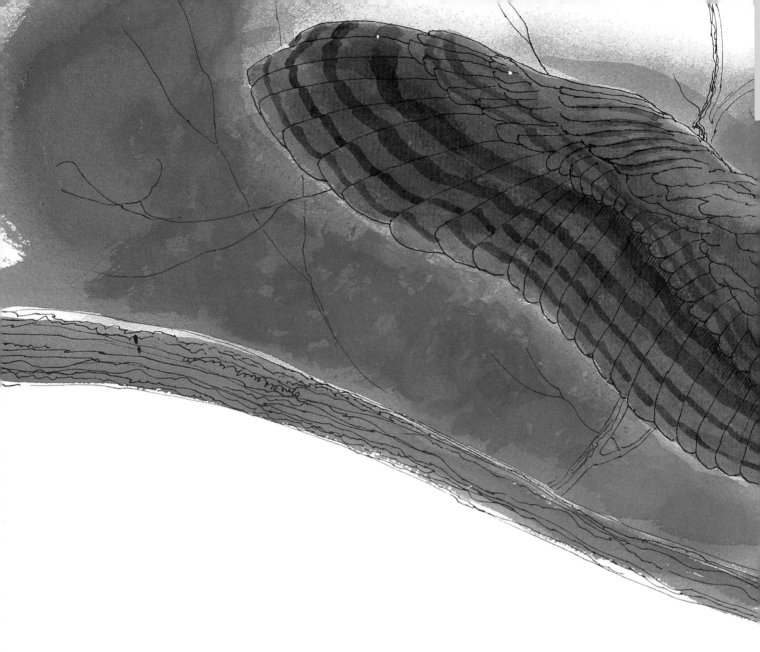

Pa turned on
his big flashlight
and caught the owl
just as it was landing
on a branch.

For one minute,
three minutes,
maybe even a hundred minutes,
we stared at one another.

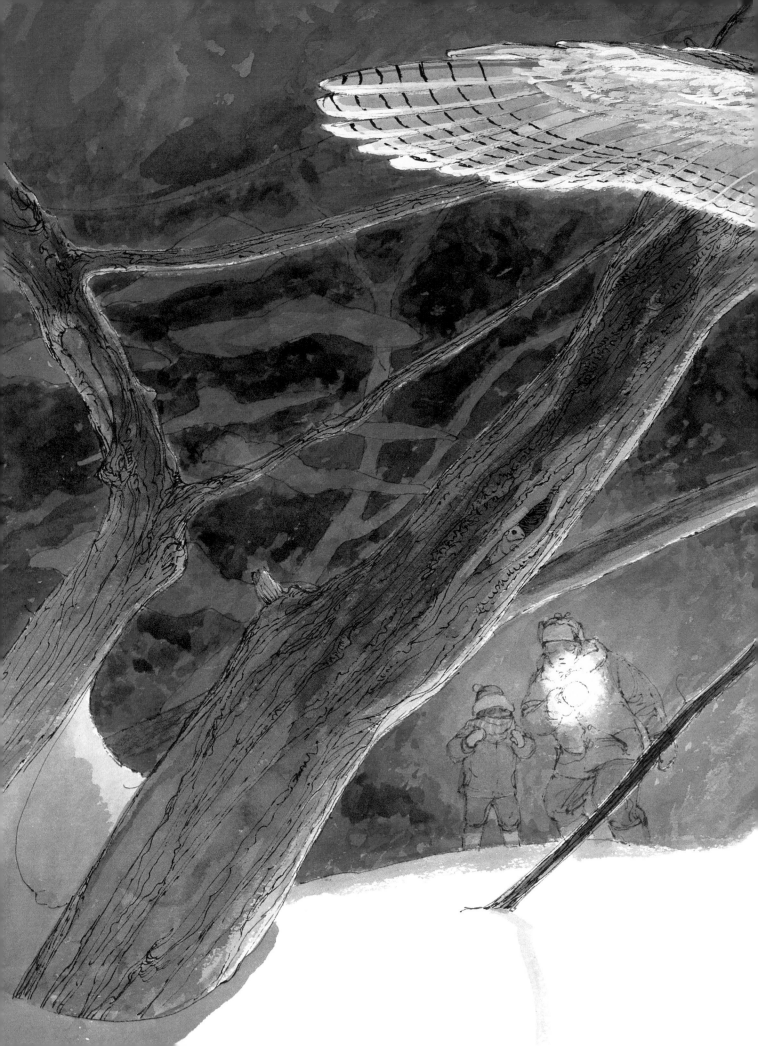

Then the owl
pumped its great wings
and lifted off the branch
like a shadow
without sound.
It flew back into the forest.
"Time to go home,"
Pa said to me.
I knew then I could talk,
I could even laugh out loud.
But I was a shadow
as we walked home.

When you go owling
you don't need words
or warm
or anything but hope.
That's what Pa says.
The kind of hope
that flies
on silent wings
under a shining
Owl Moon.